This is a Parragon book
First published in 2006

Parragon
Queen Street House
4 Queen Street
Bath, BA1 1HE, UK

ISBN 1-40547-462-9

Printed in China

Best Friends' Club

Written by Becky Brookes
Illustrated by Melanie Mitchell

Sam and Izzy had been best friends for a long time.
But the two friends were not a bit alike.

Sam liked to
climb trees
and get muddy...

...while Izzy loved wearing pretty dresses and pretending to be a prima ballerina.

It didn't seem to matter that Sam and Izzy liked different things, as long as they did them together.

At the beginning of the
summer holidays, Sam
and Izzy set up
something very special –
their own secret
Best Friends' Club.
They used the shed at
the bottom of Sam's
garden as their den,
and they decorated it
with their own
hand-made posters.

"Let's make friendship
bracelets," said Izzy,
towards the end of the
summer holidays.

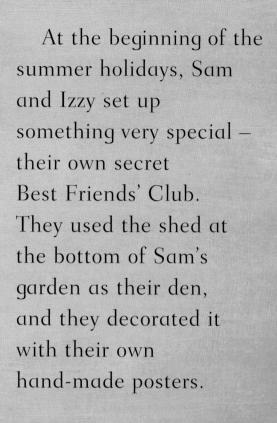

She took out some different coloured threads and began to plait them together to make a bracelet. When Izzy had finished, she placed the bracelet on Sam's wrist and tied the loose ends in a knot.

"This is for you, because you're my very best friend," she told Sam.

"Wow, thanks, Izzy," Sam grinned. "I'll make one for you too."
But Sam found it very fiddly and kept dropping the bits of thread.
"Oh, Izzy, I'm hopeless at this, could you make the bracelet for me?"

So Izzy made both bracelets and the two friends wore them every day for the rest of the summer holidays. Sam even drew a picture of them wearing their bracelets, which she gave to Izzy to keep.

On the first morning back at school, Izzy and Sam sat together in assembly. They were waiting to be put into their new classes.

"I hope we'll be put in the same class," Sam whispered to Izzy.

"Me too," Izzy whispered back.

But the two friends were put into different classes.
"We'll still be best friends though, won't we?" asked Sam, hopefully.
"Of course," Izzy smiled. "We're in the Best Friends' Club, remember?"

One morning, at breaktime, Sam couldn't wait to ask Izzy something. "Do you want to try out for the school football team with me?" she asked.

"Okay," Izzy agreed. She hadn't really thought about playing football before, but it would be great to spend more time with Sam. She missed being in the same class with her.

That lunch break, at football, Sam scored lots of goals for her team. But Izzy kept missing the ball whenever she tried to kick it.

"I'm no good at this," Izzy thought, miserably. "I wish I was doing ballet instead."

The next day, Izzy asked Sam if she wanted to go to ballet with her.

"Okay," Sam replied. She didn't really like ballet very much, but she wanted to spend more time with Izzy.

At ballet, Izzy was very graceful and dainty when she danced.

"You're a natural, Izzy," said the dance teacher.

But Sam's leotard and tutu were making her itch and she kept fidgeting and losing her balance during the warm-up positions. "I'm no good at this," Sam thought. "I wish I was playing football."

During the next few weeks, Sam and Izzy didn't see each other very much. Sam was always playing football and Izzy was often at ballet class.

Then, one morning, Sam bumped into Izzy in the cloakroom at school.

"Hi, Izzy, I haven't seen you for ages," she said.

"Well, you're always playing football," Izzy huffed, folding her arms across her chest, "and I don't like football."

"Well, you're always doing ballet," said Sam, grumpily, "and I don't like ballet."

Izzy sighed. "I thought best friends did everything together."

"Well, maybe we should stop being best friends then," Sam replied, crossly.

"Maybe we should," cried Izzy, "so I won't need to wear this any more," she said taking off her friendship bracelet before running off.

But Izzy missed Sam very much. Every night she would look at the picture Sam had drawn of them both wearing their bracelets, and she wished that everything was the way it had been in the summer.

Sam missed Izzy too. She sat in her den, their den, and thought about all the fun they'd had making up the Best Friends' Club.

"I wish I still had Izzy as my best friend," Sam thought sadly, looking at the friendship bracelet Izzy had made for her.

Just before her birthday, Izzy decided to make up with Sam. So she wrote Sam a very special party invitation.

To Sam,

Please come to my party next Saturday at 3pm.

Love from

Izzy

RSVP

P.S. Please, please, please come, Sam. I miss you lots and I want to be your best friend again.

xxx

The next day, she went to find Sam in the cloakroom at school to give her the invitation, but she couldn't see her. Suddenly a group of girls gathered around her. They were all jumping up and down with excitement.

"Thanks for the invitation to your birthday party, Izzy."

But Sam was there and overheard. Tears sprang into her eyes. "I haven't been invited to Izzy's party!" she thought sadly and rushed out of the cloakroom.

Izzy didn't see Sam. "I'll give this to Sam later," she thought, and put the invitation in her pocket.

But, in the excitement of her birthday, Izzy forgot all about giving Sam her party invitation.

The night before Izzy's birthday, Sam was very sad.

"What's wrong, Samantha?" asked her mum.

"Izzy doesn't want to be my friend any more," Sam sniffed. "She hasn't even invited me to her birthday party."

That same night, Izzy's mum was getting everything ready for Izzy's special day.

"Isn't Samantha coming to your party tomorrow?" she asked Izzy. "She hasn't replied to your invitation yet."

"Oh, no!" Izzy cried, suddenly remembering. "I forgot to give her the invitation! Sam will never want to be my friend now." And Izzy burst into tears.

"I'll give Sam's mum a call…" thought Izzy's mum.

On the day of Izzy's party, all of her friends turned up, except for Sam. Izzy was very sad. Suddenly, the doorbell went. "I think you should get that, Izzy," said her mum, with a wink. Izzy opened the front door. "Sam!" cried Izzy, giving her a hug. "I'm so sorry I forgot to give you your party invitation." "Never mind," laughed Sam. "Here, I've made a present for you. Happy Birthday, Izzy!" Izzy gently tore open the wrapping paper and gasped when she saw the beautiful friendship bracelet inside.

"It took me ages to make it," Sam blushed.

"I love it!" Izzy smiled, "does this mean that we're best friends again?"

"Always, we're in the Best Friends' Club, remember?"

And the two friends chatted and giggled as if they had never been apart!

Friendship Bracelets

Getting started

Before you start your bracelet, choose thread colours that look good together.
To start, knot the threads together at one end and tape them to a board.

Twister

This cool bracelet is the easiest to make – so get twistin'!
Choose three colours and cut three threads, 60 cm long.

1. Tie a knot 7 cm from the top, and tape the threads to your board.

2. Hold the threads together and, pulling firmly, twist them until they feel tight.

3. Hold the twist firm with one hand, and put a finger from your other hand in the middle. Now fold it up, so the ends meet.

4. Hold the ends firmly. Remove your finger, and the twisted threads will quickly wind together, leaving a loop at the bottom.

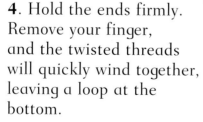

5. Take the tape off and tie a knot in the free ends at the right length. Pull the knot through the loop to fasten it round your wrist.

Well done! You've made your first bracelet.
Now try using different coloured threads and carry on plaiting!

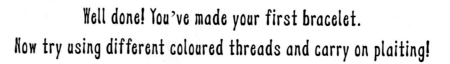

Easy-peasy Plaits

This bracelet is so quick and easy, you can make one to match every outfit!
Choose three colours and cut three lengths of each colour, about 40 cm long.

1. Knot the
threads at one
end and tape
them to your
board.

2. Separate the threads
into three colours and
spread them out in
strands. Take strand C
and cross it over strand
B. Strand C is now in
the middle.

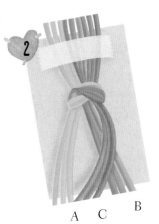

3. Now take strand A and
cross it over strand C.
Strand A is now in the
middle.

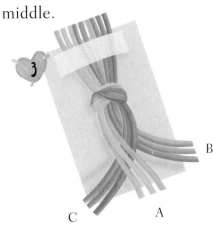

4. Continue plaiting in
the same way, right over
middle, left over middle,
until the bracelet is long
enough. Tie the ends in
a knot, then fasten it on
to your wrist.

Hot Hints
Make a thicker bracelet by using more threads.